THE 13 DAYS OF HALLOWEEN

by Carol Greene

illustrated by Tim Raglin

Troll

BridgeWater Paperback

This edition published in 2000 by BridgeWater Paperback,
an imprint and trademark of Troll Communications L.L.C.

Text copyright © 1985 by Carol Greene.

Illustrations copyright © 2000 by Tim Raglin.

Published in hardcover by BridgeWater Books.

Printed in the United States of America.

10 9 8 7 6 5 4 3 2

Library of Congress Cataloging-in-Publication Data

Greene, Carol.
    The thirteen days of Halloween / by Carol Greene; illustrated by Tim Raglin.
        p.   cm.
    Summary: A Halloween version of "The Twelve Days of Christmas," featuring such
seasonal gifts as bats, goblins, spiders, worms, and ghosts.
    ISBN 0-8167-6965-6 (lib. bdg.)   ISBN 0-8167-6980-X (pbk.)
    1. Children's songs—United States—Texts. [1. Halloween—Songs and music. 2. Songs.]
I. Raglin, Tim, ill.   II. Title.
PZ8.3.G82 Th 2000
782.42164'0268
[E]   00-023476

For Jacob Martin
—C.G.

In memory of Nelle Reneau,
teacher and friend
—T.R.

On the first day of Halloween
my good friend gave to me
a vulture in a dead tree.

On the second day of Halloween
my good friend gave to me
two hissing cats
and a vulture in a dead tree.

On the third day of Halloween
my good friend gave to me
three fat toads, two hissing cats,
and a vulture in a dead tree.

On the fourth day of Halloween
my good friend gave to me
four giggling ghosts, three fat toads,
two hissing cats,
and a vulture in a dead tree.

On the fifth day of Halloween
my good friend gave to me

five cooked worms, four giggling ghosts,
three fat toads, two hissing cats,
and a vulture in a dead tree.

On the sixth day of Halloween
my good friend gave to me

six owls a-screeching, five cooked worms,
four giggling ghosts, three fat toads,
two hissing cats,
and a vulture in a dead tree.

On the seventh day of Halloween
my good friend gave to me
seven spiders creeping, six owls a-screeching,

five cooked worms, four gigging ghosts,
three fat toads, two hissing cats,
and a vulture in a dead tree.

On the eighth day of Halloween
my good friend gave to me
eight brooms a-flying, seven spiders creeping,
six owls a-screeching, five cooked worms,
four giggling ghosts, three fat toads,
two hissing cats,
and a vulture in a dead tree.

On the ninth day of Halloween
my good friend gave to me
nine wizards whizzing, eight brooms a-flying,
seven spiders creeping, six owls a-screeching,
five cooked worms, four giggling ghosts,
three fat toads, two hissing cats,
and a vulture in a dead tree.

On the tenth day of Halloween
my good friend gave to me
ten goblins gobbling, nine wizards whizzing,
eight brooms a-flying, seven spiders creeping,
six owls a-screeching, five cooked worms,
four giggling ghosts, three fat toads,
two hissing cats,
and a vulture in a dead tree.

On the eleventh day of Halloween
my good friend gave to me
eleven bats a-swooping, ten goblins gobbling,
nine wizards whizzing, eight brooms a-flying,
seven spiders creeping, six owls a-screeching,
five cooked worms, four giggling ghosts,
three fat toads, two hissing cats,
and a vulture in a dead tree.

On the twelfth day of Halloween
my good friend gave to me . . .

twelve cauldrons bubbling, eleven bats a-swooping,
ten goblins gobbling, nine wizards whizzing,

eight brooms a-flying, seven spiders creeping,
six owls a-screeching, five cooked worms,

four giggling ghosts, three fat toads,
two hissing cats,
and a vulture in a dead tree.

On the thirteenth day of Halloween
I invited my good friend to tea,
and I gave HIM a present.

A real, live . . .

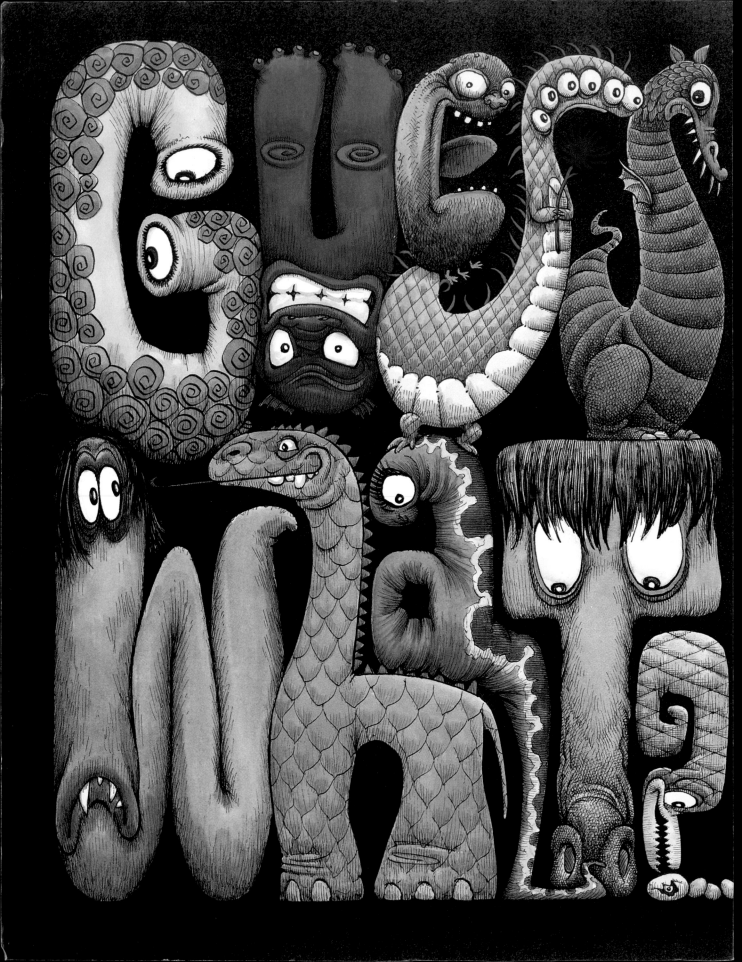